The Ghost Who Was Afraid of the Dark

by **Alex Okin**

illustrated by **Carolyn Bracken**

inchworm
PRESS ™

New York

Text copyright © 1997 Inchworm Press, a division of GT Publishing Corporation.
Illustrations copyright © 1997 Carolyn Bracken.
All rights reserved.
Designed by Lara S. Demberg.
No part of this book may be used or reproduced in any manner
whatsoever without written permission from the publisher.
For information address Inchworm Press,
16 East 40th Street, New York, New York 10016.

In a big old house on top of a hill there lived a young ghost named Spookie. Spookie and his parents lived in the attic. A human family lived in the rest of the house. Spookie was allowed out of the attic only in the daytime because he was too young to spook at night.

During the day Spookie liked to float from one bright, sunny room to another. His favorite places to visit were the children's rooms. He would play with their dolls and trucks and stuffed animals while they were at school. Sometimes he forgot to put the toys away — but usually he remembered.

One afternoon when Spookie returned to the attic, his mother said, "It's time you learned how to haunt at night, dear."

"Really?" said Spookie, feeling a bit nervous. "But don't
ou think the night is too dark for a little ghost like me?"
  "You've grown quite a bit this past year," said his father.
It's time you act like a big ghost and learn how to scare
ie humans at night."

"And remember, dear, at night we get to wear our chains and rattle them around when we haunt," said his mother.

"But I'm not used to the dark," said Spookie. "I've never even stayed up past sunset."

"Big ghosts don't sleep at night, dear," his mother said. "You'll get used to the dark."

That night when the coast was clear, Spookie followed his parents through the attic door. The house was dark and still, and the humans were asleep in their beds.

"Follow us," said Spookie's father. "We'll show you the best places to hide and haunt."

They drifted into the musty old library. "I'm scared," Spookie whispered. "It's too dark in here."

"Shhh," said his mother. "You'll be okay."

But Spookie couldn't keep quiet. Before he knew it, he was crying, "Boo-hoo! Boo-hoo!" Suddenly the ghosts heard a door open upstairs. Then they heard the humans moving around.

"Quick, Spookie, hide behind these curtains," said his mother. Spookie's parents began to blow with all their might. The howling of their voices masked the sound of Spookie's cries. The curtains flapped loudly in the breeze.

"Not to worry. It's just the wind," said a voice upstairs. Soon the humans were quiet again.

When they were back in the light of the hallway, Spookie's father whispered, "Now Spookie, I want you to float into the little girl's bedroom and hide in her toy closet."

"But what if I knock something over? What if I start to cry and I wake everyone up?" Spookie asked.

"You'll be fine. The dark is not going to hurt you," said his mother.

Spookie dashed through the door of the little girl's bedroom, and let out a sigh of relief when he saw that she slept with a tiny night-light on.

The toy closet was the darkest place he had ever been in by himself. Spookie shook so much with fear that his chains began to rattle. He tried hard not to cry, but he just couldn't help himself. Finally he whimpered, "Boo-hoo! Boo-hoo!"

The little girl woke up and started to cry, too. The sound surprised Spookie because when the little girl cried, she sounded just like him!

The little girl's parents rushed into her room. "Why are you crying, dear?" they asked her.

"There's a ghost in my room!" cried the little girl.

"There, there. You must have been dreaming," said her parents as they tucked her back into bed.

"I want my dolly," the little girl said. "I can't go back to sleep without my dolly."

"Where *is* your dolly?" her mother asked.

The little girl looked sad. "I don't know," she said. "She's lost."

The mother went into the toy closet to look for the doll.
Spookie quietly floated up and out of the closet, over her
head. She didn't even see him.

When the little girl's mother couldn't find the doll anywhere, she picked up a stuffed bear. "How about sleeping with Fuzzy instead?"

The little girl shook her head. "I want my dolly."

Suddenly Spookie remembered that he had been playing with the doll earlier that day. He must have forgotten to put it back where it belonged.

"I'll get it!" he whispered to himself.

Spookie floated under the little girl's bed where the doll was lying. Luckily the little girl's parents were so busy comforting her that they didn't notice him.

Spookie carefully pushed the doll out from under the bed until it was laying beside the mother's foot.

"Oh, here she is," exclaimed the mother a moment later.

"Thank you, Mommy!" cried the little girl, hugging the
doll. "I'm so happy you found her."

Me, too, thought Spookie. Hearing the little girl's happy
voice made Spookie forget to be afraid of the darkness
under the bed.

Back in the attic, Spookie told his parents that when he was under the little girl's bed he wasn't afraid of the dark at all.

"We're very proud of you, dear," said his mother. "Now that you're not afraid of the dark anymore you can haunt with us every night."

Spookie snuggled against his soft quilt, and felt very grown-up. He didn't want to spook at night. He wanted to help people instead. "That will be my special secret," he whispered out loud. Then he drifted off to sleep.